THE UNDERDOGS

EVAN JACOBS

BEHIND THE MASK	IGGY	SCRATCH N' SNITCH
BREAK AND ENTER	ON THE RUN	SUMMER CAMP
EMOJI OF DOOM	QWIK CUTTER	**THE UNDERDOGS**
GRAND SLAM	REBEL	UNDER THE STAIRS

Copyright © 2017 by Saddleback Educational Publishing

All rights reserved. No part of this book may be reproduced in any form or by any means, electronic or mechanical, including photocopying, recording, scanning, or by any information storage and retrieval system, without the written permission of the publisher. SADDLEBACK EDUCATIONAL PUBLISHING and any associated logos are trademarks and/or registered trademarks of Saddleback Educational Publishing.

ISBN-13: 978-1-68021-144-3
ISBN-10: 1-68021-144-7
eBook: 978-1-63078-543-7

Printed in Malaysia

21 20 19 18 17   1 2 3 4 5

GIRLS' TACKLE FOOTBALL STATS

UTAH HAS THE COUNTRY'S FIRST TACKLE FOOTBALL TEAM FOR 5TH & 6TH GRADE GIRLS

HOW MANY GIRLS IN THE SCHOOL WANT TO PLAY COED FOOTBALL

|||| |||| ||

BOYS THINK GIRLS CAN'T PLAY BECAUSE...

THEY WILL [cry] & GET [hurt]

THINK AGAIN, BOYS!

CHAPTER 1

LUNCH GAME

Jasmine Le's eyes narrowed. She was watching Mark Kline play football. It was lunchtime. Mark and some other guys were playing.

A blond thirteen-year-old god. Wow! she thought.

"Oh man!" Mark yelled. "You blew it."

He was looking at Mike Ramirez. Mike had missed a pass. The ball was on the ground. It had landed close to Jasmine.

Her BFFs were sitting on some bleachers behind her. Zoe Ebad and Tess Quade. Zoe was a tall and perfect blonde. "Do you ever get pimples? I've never seen one on your face. Unfair!" Tess once told her.

Tess's hair was long and brown. She had smooth dark skin.

Jasmine was a hybrid of the two. Long black hair. Olive skin.

Everyone on the field was in eighth grade. They went to Meadow Springs Middle School.

"Shouldn't you throw the ball back?" Zoe asked.

Jasmine wasn't a tomboy. But there were only boys on her street. She had played kickball with them. Baseball, soccer, and even tackle football too. She grabbed the football. Then she threw it back.

"Oh my gosh!" Zoe said, laughing. "You did it. I can't believe it."

"Did you think she wouldn't?" Tess asked.

Chapter 1

The ball soared through the air. The boys watched it. Mark barely moved to catch it.

"Nice throw," Mark said. "For a girl."

"Nice throw, period," Jasmine said.

Mark laughed. "All right. Let's get in our formations," he called. "We still have fifteen minutes till the bell rings."

"Are you going to eat your lunch?" Zoe asked. She held up Jasmine's sandwich. "It looks good."

"Eat it," Jasmine said. "I'm going to play football."

Tess and Zoe looked at each other. "I don't recall them asking you to play," Tess said.

"So?" Jasmine smirked. She walked out onto the field. Jasmine planted herself between the two teams. The boys started yelling. She tuned it out. Mark stared at her. She didn't even blink.

"What are you doing?" Mark asked.

"I want to play football," Jasmine said. "I'm just as good as any of you."

"But you're a girl." Mark frowned. "You can't play football!"

"Why not? I play with boys a lot. I've even played tackle football."

"You're a girl!" Mark said again. "You will get hurt."

"No, I won't!"

The other boys yelled too. They told Jasmine to get off the field. Tess and Zoe ran over.

"Jasmine," Zoe said. "Come on!"

"Ignore our friend," Tess said to Mark. "She ate lunch in the cafeteria. Bad food makes you weird."

"I'm feeling fine," Jasmine said. "If boys can play football, we can too."

"Mr. Ross," the boys called.

Mr. Ross was in charge of school security. The man was short and stocky. He always wore tracksuits. Maybe he had played high school football. But he was out of shape now.

"What's the problem here?" Mr. Ross asked.

Chapter 1

"Jasmine thinks she can get in on this game. Play football with us," Mark said.

"I *can* play football," Jasmine said. "They just won't let me."

Mr. Ross stared at them. "Um. Now listen, Jasmine." Mr. Ross stopped talking. He looked like he was thinking. "These boys are playing football. It's not the game for you."

"Why not?"

"Well. Um … because you're a girl."

"That's not a reason. Sex doesn't matter. I can play," Jasmine insisted.

"Get her off the field, Mr. Ross!" one player yelled.

"Look," Mr. Ross said. "You must get off—"

"No!"

Silence.

Mr. Ross was known for being nice. But he did have a temper. "Leave this field, or go see the principal. It's up to you."

Jasmine held her ground. But Zoe stepped

in. "We were just leaving," she said. Zoe grabbed Jasmine's arm. "Enjoy your game," she yelled to the boys.

Tess grabbed Jasmine's other arm.

The girls led her off the field.

The rest of lunch passed in silence. Jasmine sat on the bleachers with Tess and Zoe. She watched the game. What would it be like if she were allowed to play?

"Stop being so mad," Zoe said. "You want to play football? Since when?"

"Since those boys wouldn't let me," Jasmine said.

Jasmine fumed the rest of the day. No way would she take no for an answer. Girls could play football. They could if they wanted to play.

The friends met up after school. They always walked home together.

"Look," Tess said. "That shirt is so cute." Tess

showed the girls her phone. The cool shirt was on Instagram.

"Do you like it, Jazz?" Tess asked Jasmine.

Jasmine eyed the shirt. It was white. "I'm Not Hot" was written on it. "It's cool," Jasmine said.

But Jasmine kept thinking about football. Zoe and Tess talked. Jasmine thought about justice. Then something caught her eye. They were near Wagner Park.

There was Mark. Again. It was football practice. Looked like a Pop Warner team. She could see the team name. The Marauders.

Their coach was tall. He was dressed like Mr. Ross.

Jasmine had a thought. "Wait! I've got an idea," she said. She walked over to the field.

"Here we go again," Zoe said, rolling her eyes.

CHAPTER 2

PASS

"You want to do what?" Coach Sanderson asked. He was the coach of the Marauders.

Jasmine was standing on the field. Coach Sanderson was in front of her. There were players on both sides of them.

"I want to play football. On this team."

"But …" Coach Sanderson was confused. "You're a girl."

"So," Jasmine said. Was that his only argument?

"Don't worry about her, Coach," Mark called. He was standing at the front of the blocking line. "She did this at school today too. She thinks she can play tackle football."

"And why can't I? I've played with boys since I was five. I'm thirteen now."

"Listen, little lady," Coach Sanderson said.

"I'm not a 'little lady.' I'm a young lady," Jasmine said fiercely. She was mad. Mr. Ross had talked to her the same way.

Jasmine knew there were differences between boys and girls. She knew there were things they both couldn't do. She just didn't understand why she couldn't play football.

"Well, *young lady*, leave the field." Coach Sanderson glared at her. "Football is a man's game. When you get to high school, you can be a cheerleader. Then you can be on the field. Cheer these boys on."

The boys started laughing. Then they yelled at her. Told her to forget about it.

Coach Sanderson didn't do anything.

Jasmine walked off the field.

"I'm going to play this game!" Jasmine called. She knew they thought she was crazy. She didn't care. "You watch!"

"Get a team together. Then we'll talk," Coach Sanderson said.

"You mean it?" Jasmine stopped walking and turned.

Coach Sanderson didn't say more. He nodded his head, then waved them off.

Jasmine looked at Mark. He stared at her with a confused expression. Jasmine was grinning now. Coach Sanderson had said yes. All Jasmine had to do was get a team together.

Jasmine walked over to her friends. "He said yes," she said. "You guys heard him, right?"

"Are you sure he meant it?" Zoe asked. "Looked like he blew you off."

"Who cares how it looked." Jasmine was excited. "We need to get a team together."

"We?" Tess asked. "I don't know how to play football."

"Don't worry," Jasmine said. "I'll teach you."

"If they really let us play," Zoe said. "We could get hurt."

"Oh, they'll let us play," Jasmine said. "And we won't get hurt."

"So all you have to do is form a team?" Jasmine's mom asked.

They were sitting in Applebee's. A waiter served turkey burgers and fries.

Jasmine looked like a mini-version of her mom. They had the same long black hair. Their olive skin was smooth and flawless.

"Yeah," Jasmine said, taking a sip of water. "Tess and Zoe didn't think he was serious. He sounded real to me."

"Then that's all that matters, right?" Her mom smiled.

"Yeah."

Jasmine and her mom were close. They liked to shop together. Jasmine did things with her mom on the weekends. Mother and daughter were very close.

Jasmine's dad had died three years before. He'd had cancer. The three of them had been tight.

"It's odd. Why won't they let you play with the boys?" Her mom took a bite. "There's a girls' tackle football league in Arizona."

"Ugh. I don't know. But it doesn't matter now. I'm going to put together a girls' team. We're going to kick their butts!"

"Don't you want your team to be coed?" her mom asked. "The point of this was to be inclusive, right?"

"It was." Jasmine ate a few fries. "But they made it about me being a girl. Coach said that was why I couldn't play. So now I'm going to form my own team. We'll beat the boys. That will show them never to dismiss girls again. *Then* I'll play on their stupid team."

"Right on!" Her mom held up her hand.

Jasmine gave her a high five.

"I know you, Jasmine. You always figure out a way. You're determined. You get that from your awesome dad."

CHAPTER 3

KICKOFF

"What are you saying?" Zoe asked. "We need eight other girls?"

"Yes," Jasmine said. "We need at least eleven players on the field. Even more would be better."

It was lunchtime. The girls walked around school. Students were texting. Others did homework. More gathered in groups and talked.

Jasmine hoped to put the team together. Lunch was a key time. The earlier morning break was too short. Jasmine wanted to recruit the girls. Then she would take them to the field. She wanted to show her team to the boys.

"Do we even know eight other girls?" Tess asked.

"Eight other girls. Yeah. Girls who want to play football? Not so much," Zoe said.

"Don't we need a coach?" Tess asked.

"We'll find the girls." Jasmine smiled. "I'm not worried about it. As for a coach? We are going to do it."

"How?" Tess and Zoe asked at the same time.

"I know how to play football." Jasmine checked out the students. She was trying to spot girls they knew. Girls who could be on the team. "A coach would want us to do things their way. We need to do this our way. How sweet will it be when we beat those lame boys?"

"They're not all lame," Zoe said.

"I hate to say it. Mark is kind of cute," Tess said.

"Ew," Jasmine said. She was furious with Mark. Even thinking about the boys made her mad. Their bad attitudes sucked.

Chapter 3

Just then Jo-Jo Williams walked by. Jo-Jo had been into sports since forever. She was a big girl. Jo-Jo had always been taller than most kids. She was also a knockout. Blonde. Fair. Strong.

"Well," Jasmine said. "Time to put our team together."

"Jo-Jo!" Tess called.

Jo-Jo turned. She looked around. "Who called me?" she asked.

Tess, Jasmine, and Zoe waved at her.

Jo-Jo walked over. "What's up?" She smiled. "I haven't talked to you guys since fifth grade."

Fifth grade. That was the last grade of elementary school. Sixth, seventh, and eighth grades were middle school. A lot had changed since then.

"We wanted to know something. Do you want to be on our football team?" Jasmine asked.

"You guys are starting a football team? At school?" Jo-Jo's eyes widened.

"Well, we'll practice after school. Nobody will let girls play football. Not here. Not after school. Nowhere. A tackle football coach told us we could play against his team. We just have to put our team together."

"Whoa! I'm in," Jo-Jo said. She held up her hand for a high five.

"Great!" Jasmine said. "Meet us out front after school. We're going to walk to the park. The Marauders play there. That's the boys' team we're going to play. I want to show them we're serious."

"See you then, Captain!" Jo-Jo punched Jasmine in the shoulder. Then she walked away.

"Wow!" Zoe said.

"That was easy," Tess said.

"Ladies …" Jasmine was practically glowing now. "We just need seven more girls!"

Next they talked with Ashlan Hwang. She was tall with short brown hair. She was also one of the smartest girls at school.

"Football?" Ashlan asked. She pushed up her glasses. "Newsflash. I'm a nerd."

"What does that matter?" Jasmine asked.

Chapter 3

"Who says football players can't be super smart?"

"And beautiful?" Tess added.

"Yeah," Zoe said.

"Um, I don't know," Ashlan said. "Can I say maybe?"

"Sure." Jasmine started to walk away. "Just meet us out front after school."

"Okay," Ashlan said, confused.

"Jazz," Zoe said. "Ashlan didn't exactly say yes."

"But she didn't say no."

Tess led them to Kendra and Kim Chavez. The sisters were identical twins. Sometimes they even dressed the same.

Tess explained the situation. "What do you girls say?" she asked. "Want to play tackle football against a bunch of boys?"

"Yes!" Kendra and Kim said in unison.

"See?" Tess turned to Jasmine and Zoe. "Aren't they perfect?"

"They sure are," Jasmine agreed.

The team now had seven players. The girls just needed four more.

Jasmine, Zoe, and Tess continued to comb the school. Then Becky Turner came up to them. Jasmine's eyes got wide. Tess and Zoe gasped.

Becky was the toughest girl at school. She had transferred there the year before. She was a seventh grader. But she had a big reputation.

Why did she transfer? Nobody knew. Had she fought with a teacher? Beat up a kid for laughing? It was anyone's guess.

Becky was short. Her muscles were fierce. She always wore black. Her brown hair was short and spiky.

"You three starting a football team? That's what I hear," Becky said. She gave Jasmine no personal space. Her eyes burned into them.

"Yes, Becky." Jasmine smiled nervously. "We are."

"No you're not." Becky cracked her knuckles.

It was loud. "You haven't asked me to be on it. So it's not a team yet."

Jasmine stared into Becky's blue eyes. Was Becky tough on purpose? Did she just want to belong? Maybe people listened only when she acted scary.

"Will you work hard? Attend all the practices?" Jasmine asked. She tried to sound stern.

"Of course," Becky said. "I love football."

"Perfect!" Jasmine said. "We need all the players we can get. Welcome to the team!"

Becky's frown turned into a warm smile. Before Jasmine knew it, Becky hugged her. "Great! Thanks a lot, Jasmine! When do we practice? When's our first game?"

"Well," Jasmine said. "Meet us out front after school. We need to talk to the boys' coach. They practice at Wagner Park. That team will be our first victim."

"Oh, cool!" Becky punched her fist into her

hand. "I love hitting boys! Now I can do it and not get in trouble!" Becky cackled as she walked away.

Zoe took out her cellphone. She was keeping a log of names. "Well, now we have Becky. That means we've got eight players."

"Great!" Jasmine was excited. This was really happening. She was putting together a football team.

"Don't we need at least three more?" Tess asked.

"We'll get them later," Jasmine said.

The bell rang. Lunch was over. Students started walking to their classes.

"Aren't we going over to the park after school?" Zoe asked. "I thought you wanted to show the coach we had a full team."

"It'll be fine." Jasmine was too excited. She didn't care that her team was missing players. "It's not like we're going to play the boys today."

CHAPTER 4

SACK

"I still think we should have all eleven players," Zoe said. "We want Coach Sanderson and the boys to take us seriously."

"Stop being so negative," Jasmine snapped. "I want to get a date set up. We're going to need to practice a lot. The more prepared we are the better."

The eight-player team walked down the street. Jasmine, Zoe, and Tess were in front. Kendra and Kim were next. Jo-Jo and Becky followed. The two discussed the kind of weights they lifted.

Ashlan was last. She was playing *Geometry Wars 3: Dimensions Evolved* on her phone.

"Hey, Zoe!" a voice called.

Jasmine, Tess, and Zoe looked around. It was Emma, Zoe's sister. She was only ten. Emma was a fifth grader. She looked just like her big sister.

"Go away, Emma," Zoe said, rolling her eyes.

"Why? I just wanted to walk home with you," Emma whined.

"We're doing big-girl stuff," Tess said. She checked her phone messages. "You wouldn't understand."

"I am a big girl," Emma said.

Becky and Jo-Jo laughed.

"Emma," Zoe said through gritted teeth. "If you don't go home right now—"

"Don't go home!" Jasmine said, cutting her off.

"What?" Zoe couldn't believe it. What was Jasmine saying? The girls never wanted her little sister around. "You want Emma to stay?"

"You said it. We're short players," Jasmine said. "We need all the help we can get."

"Hah!" Emma yelled.

"I said we're short players. Not that we need short players," Zoe said.

"I'm not short!" Emma said. "Mom says I may be taller than you someday!"

"Whatever," Zoe said. She took out her phone. Then scrolled through it.

Jasmine couldn't help but smile. They were acting like a team. Already! Kids on teams teased each other. They had fun.

This is awesome!

Jasmine could tell something was wrong. The girls marched toward the boys' practice. She didn't like what she saw.

Boys were pointing at them and laughing. Coach Sanderson looked confused.

Jasmine realized she had misread Coach

Sanderson. No way was he letting the girls play. He didn't think she could put a team together.

"What is this?" The coach frowned as they got closer.

"You told us to put a team together." Jasmine smiled confidently. "Well, here's our team."

The coach looked at the girls. So did his team. "You're two players short." Coach Sanderson turned around. He talked to his team. "All right, here's what's next—"

"Wait!" Jasmine yelled. "That's what you said. And we did it. We put a team together."

"Everyone heard you," Zoe said.

The boys looked at their coach. Coach turned. He stared at the girls. "Look …" He tried to smile. "You're all cute. Girls and boys aren't meant to play football together. You're just not built for it."

"We can play football," Becky yelled. "We can take it."

"Yeah," Jasmine said. "And you said—"

"Listen!" Coach Sanderson yelled. "I'm trying to coach here."

"We just want to play football," Emma said.

The boys laughed.

"Look at that, Coach," Mark said. "Even their half-pint player has a big mouth."

"Shut up!" Jasmine cried. "You boys are just scared."

"Enough!" Coach Sanderson walked toward Jasmine. "If you girls don't leave now, I'm calling the police."

Jasmine stared at the football coach. Then she looked at her crew. "Call them," Jasmine said. "They need to know you're a liar."

And that's exactly what Coach did. It was a few minutes later. Jasmine sat in a police car. She had told her friends to leave. "It's for the team," she had said. "We can't all be arrested."

Officer Villa was the neighborhood top cop. Everybody knew him. He looked mean but was really nice. Officer Villa drove Jasmine to her house.

"She's not in any trouble," Officer Villa told Jasmine's mom.

Jasmine walked into the house. She stood next to her mom.

Officer Villa stood on the porch.

"Oh, good! I'm glad." Jasmine's mom laughed. "I about had a heart attack when I saw your patrol car."

"Keep her away from Wagner Park. At least while the team is practicing," Officer Villa said.

"You got it." She looked at Jasmine. "Right?"

"I don't have a choice," Jasmine said.

Jasmine and her mom lived in a small one-story house. They decorated for each season. Right now it was fall. The house felt extra cozy.

Jasmine walked into the kitchen. She heard the front door close. Jasmine grabbed a banana. Her mom followed her into the kitchen.

"I hate that coach!" Jasmine said. She was

angry. "How dare he diss our team. We deserve to play."

"Did you think this would be easy?" Jasmine's mom smiled.

"What should I do?" Jasmine asked. She took a bite of banana.

"Here's what you shouldn't do," Jasmine's mom said. She started to set the table. "Don't back down. Figure out how to play. But don't get in trouble. Be polite. Respectful."

"That might be kind of hard."

"Jasmine …" Her mother poured some water into glasses. "Nothing that's worth anything is easy."

It was the next day. Tess, Zoe, and Jasmine were walking to class.

"What?" Jasmine asked.

"Is this worth it? Football is getting you in trouble," Zoe said.

"Yeah," Tess agreed.

"Don't you guys see? This isn't about football." Jasmine saw Mark. He was talking with some football players. "We must stand up to the boys. Or nothing's going to change."

"We know you, Jazz," Zoe said. "You get excited about stuff. You want everybody else to be excited too. We're just being the voice of reason."

"We need to tell you the truth," Tess said. "That's what friends do."

"So you guys aren't going to play?" Jasmine's eyes were moist.

Mark walked over to them.

"Hey, Jasmine," he said. "About your team. We want to play you guys."

"Who?" Jasmine asked. She took a deep breath. Mark could not see how upset she was.

"My entire team. Duh."

"I thought your coach—"

"Coach Sanderson doesn't need to know about it. Oh, we'll beat you. Then you girls have to knock off this football stuff."

Jasmine eyed Zoe and Tess.

See! she wanted to say. *This is how boys think! They don't think girls can do anything.*

"Why can't we play?" Tess asked.

"Because football is for boys," Mark said.

"No way. It isn't!" Zoe said.

Jasmine couldn't help but smile. Zoe and Tess looked at her. Girls could do anything.

"Let's play them, Jasmine," Zoe said.

"Who cares if we get in trouble?" Tess said.

"Okay! We'll agree to not play football. But only if we lose." Jasmine turned back to Mark. "And when we win? You have to tell Coach Sanderson girls belong on your team. He might say no. But you'll tell him you won't play unless the team is coed."

"You're crazy, but okay," Mark said.

"Will all the guys agree?" Jasmine asked.

"Yep," Mark said. "Because girls beating boys? Never going to happen. Just keep your promise. No. More. Football."

CHAPTER 5

PRACTICE

Zoe and Tess were standing with their crew. It included Becky, Ashlan, Kendra, Kim, and Jo-Jo. The girls were at Gomez Field. To call it a field was a joke. Most of the grass was dead.

The girls were standing in two rows. Jasmine was facing them. They were doing jumping jacks. It was the last warm-up stretch.

The girls were stiff. Uncoordinated. Out of shape. The jumping jacks were a disaster. Then there were push-ups. The girls were unsteady. Forget about crunches. Everyone groaned.

Except Jo-Jo. She was the only fit girl.

"One last warm-up, girls. Laps. Let's do four around the field," Jasmine said.

Jo-Jo nodded her head with enthusiasm. The other girls looked miserable.

"Do we have to?" Tess asked. "Can't we just go right to the plays? I think I'm too sore to run."

Many of the girls seconded Tess.

"You guys …" Jasmine tried not to sound exasperated. "Our game is in a month. Do you think the Marauders are complaining? No! They are training. We have to get into shape. Otherwise we will lose and lose big."

Jasmine took off. Gomez Field was large. No way could they run four laps.

"Jasmine!" Emma called. She caught up to Jasmine. There were two girls with her. "This is Alejandra and Lisa. They want to be on the team."

Jasmine looked at them. Were they younger

than Emma? She thought so. "How old are you?" Jasmine asked.

"Nine," Alejandra said.

"Ten," Lisa said.

Jasmine stared. Ugh! This was bad news.

"You said we needed two more players," Emma said. "Here they are."

"Well …" Jasmine closed her eyes. "All right. At least we have a full team now."

Jasmine stopped running. She had the girls split up. Five on one side. Six on the other side.

She explained a play. It looked like everyone understood. One side would play defense. The other would play offense.

Jasmine's side didn't get far. Becky and Jo-Jo collided. Then they started pushing each other. Later, Zoe kept dropping the ball. Kendra tackled Kim. But they were on the same side!

Jasmine had wanted to practice plays for two hours. She stopped the girls after thirty minutes.

CHAPTER 6

HOPELESS

It was a week later. Two boys walked past Jasmine. One was Tyler Prescott. The other, Gabriel Aron. Both played for the Marauders.

"Girls," Tyler said.

"Can't play," Gabriel continued.

"Football," Tyler finished.

They high-fived each other. Tyler and Gabriel eyed Jasmine.

"Wow! Clever. Think of that by yourselves?" Jasmine asked. "I'm impressed."

"Whatever," Tyler said.

"Whatever nothing," Jasmine said. "We *will* beat you guys."

"Three more weeks. Then you and your girlies are dead meat," Gabriel said.

Just then Mark walked up. The guys high-fived him. Mark smiled.

Jasmine wanted to say more. But what would it matter? The real talking would happen on the field.

Jasmine went into that afternoon's practice even more determined. So far the team was bad.

We have to get better!

But at Gomez Field it was no better. The girls sucked. They had problems exercising. Except for Jo-Jo. She never got tired.

Jasmine tried to run more plays. But it was more of the same. A big mess. Ashlan intercepted the ball. But she ran in the wrong direction.

"You guys," Jasmine yelled. "We've been

practicing that play. We've done it every day for more than a week!"

The girls stopped. They looked at her. Jasmine was frustrated. She also seemed mad.

"You guys are hopeless! And you're playing hopeless. Acting hopeless. Argh! Maybe we shouldn't do this." Then she turned and stormed off.

CHAPTER 7

INTERCEPTION

Jasmine thought she would feel better. She had spoken her mind. Her brain told her to go back to the field. Her body kept walking.

That's when she ran into Mark. He was across the street. He was in his football uniform. It was black and white.

He looks a lot older than thirteen, Jasmine thought. *Is it because of the uniform?*

He crossed the street. Then walked toward her.

"How's practice going?" he asked.

"Oh, like you care," she snapped. Would he ever know they were terrible? She wasn't going to give him the satisfaction. "You want us to fail. It's a boys' club."

"Hey, I'm sorry about what happened at school," he said. "I didn't hear what those guys said."

"But you high-fived them anyway. You knew they were being disrespectful. All of you are disrespectful to girls."

"Come on. I said I was sorry." Mark smiled.

"Whatever!"

Jasmine continued walking. Mark walked with her.

"Football's a tough game," he said.

"I know that!" Jasmine shot back.

"But you girls are determined. I know how I am at school. I know how I am in front of the guys. But …" Mark looked at the ground. "Honestly, I'd be surprised if you hadn't put a team together. You really believe you can do this."

"Don't you believe you can play?" Jasmine asked.

"Yeah."

"Then why shouldn't I? Because I'm a girl? Because football's for boys?"

"Well, I still think it is." Mark looked at Jasmine. He wasn't smiling. "Maybe you'll prove me wrong."

Jasmine couldn't help but smile. Maybe Mark wasn't so bad.

"I doubt it, though." Mark grinned.

"Something on your mind?" Jasmine's mom asked. She was standing in the doorway of Jasmine's room. Jasmine was sitting on her bed. It was bedtime. She had been reading. Then she started thinking.

I suck. I can't believe how I acted today.

"I yelled at my team today," Jasmine said. "I feel terrible. Coaching is hard and frustrating."

"Well, you're a big person. Sometimes that's what it takes to say you're sorry."

"Yeah, you're right, Mom."

"Coaching people may not always be fun. But try to make it more fun. Maybe things will go better."

CHAPTER 8

FUNBALL

Zoe and Tess looked at Jasmine. They held their phones. Jasmine felt nervous. She walked toward her two besties.

"I'm so sorry, you guys," Jasmine said before they could speak. "I was such a jerk yesterday."

"It's okay," Zoe said.

"Yeah. We've known you a long time. We're used to you acting cray-cray. At least from time to time." Tess smiled.

They hugged each other.

"You just get so focused, Jazz," Zoe said. "There's nothing wrong with it. Sometimes your passion is too deep. You want us to be this great football team. Most of us have never touched a football."

"I know," Jasmine said. "I lost my mind. It's just ... I want to beat those boys. They think we're losers."

"We both want to support you," Tess said.

"Yeah," Zoe said. "But this team needs to be more fun."

"It will be." Jasmine grinned. "I promise."

The bell sounded for first period.

"You think everyone will come back?" Jasmine asked nervously.

"I don't know, Jazz," Tess said. "You were pretty harsh."

They started walking to class.

"You two will be at practice today, right?" Jasmine was scared. She wanted everyone to be there. But she needed Zoe and Tess. Without them there was no team. No matter how good or bad they were.

"Of course," Zoe said. "We're you're best friends."

After school Jasmine, Zoe, and Tess were waiting at Gomez Field. Practice was at three. It was three fifteen. Nobody else had arrived yet.

"I guess we need new teammates," Jasmine said glumly.

"Yeah, maybe," Zoe said.

Then Ashlan appeared. She was in her PE clothes. Ashlan was so skinny. How was she going to crush it at football? But she looked confident as she walked toward them.

"Hey," Jasmine said. "You came back."

"Yeah, of course. Why wouldn't I?" Ashlan asked. "I'm still on the team, right?"

"You bet you are!" Jasmine said.

"The other girls are coming." Ashlan motioned to them.

Jasmine looked over. There they were. Becky. Kendra. Kim. Jo-Jo. Emma. Alejandra. Lisa. They were dressed and ready for practice.

CHAPTER 9

SNAP

It was a few days later. Jasmine watched the team move down the field. They were still clumsy. Zoe and Tess tried running a play. They both froze during the action.

Becky was great at charging down the field. Blocking was no problem. She just wasn't fast.

Ashlan was not as timid as Jasmine thought she would be. She was fast. And not easily intimidated. It was a sweet surprise.

"We'll begin with touch football," Jasmine

said. "We can tackle a little. But I don't want anyone getting hurt."

"What about when we play the boys?" Tess asked.

"Well, I don't think we'll have a problem tackling them," Jasmine said. "And they certainly won't have a problem tackling us."

Jo-Jo was a good athlete. She had even tackled a few of the girls. Nobody had gotten hurt.

Despite being twins, Kendra and Kim had different talents. Kendra was fast. Jasmine wanted her to be a wide receiver. And Kim? She was born to kick.

As for Emma, Alejandra, and Lisa? For small girls they were great at blocking.

"The boys will probably underestimate you," Jasmine said. "We can use that to our advantage."

During most plays, Jasmine divided the team. It was five against six. Each side tried to gain control of the ball.

After practice Jasmine gathered the girls.

"You guys, we are starting to look like a

team," Jasmine said. "There's work to do. We need to get our plays down. Let's start tackling. But we need to be safe about it. It's so cool! We're a team."

Jo-Jo cheered. Then Becky. Tess. Zoe. Ashlan. And finally the other girls.

Everyone started walking home. Jasmine was with her besties.

"I like playing football. It's great. I never thought it would be so fun," Zoe said.

"I said you would," Jasmine said.

"Well, chicas," Tess said. "It's been real. See you both later." She turned down her street.

"Tess, wait up. I need to get my iPad," Zoe said. "I left it at your house."

"Oh yeah."

"Later, Jazzy." Zoe followed Tess.

"See you tomorrow," Jasmine called.

She continued walking down the street. A few minutes later she saw Mark on the other side. He was in his football uniform. He smiled self-consciously. Then walked over to her.

"Are you stalking me?" Jasmine asked, teasing.

"No!" Mark laughed. "You just always walk home this way. I think you're stalking me."

"Soon we'll be walking home together. We'll play on the same team. After my girls beat your guys!" Did she sound like she was interested in him? She hadn't meant to.

"You know what your problem is," Mark said. "You think everything is a fight. It isn't. I saw you walking on the other side of the street. I wanted to walk over. So I did."

"Why?"

"Well, it wasn't to argue," Mark said.

"You started it." Jasmine tried to sound playful. "Saying all that stuff at school."

"Yeah, maybe you're right."

"I am. Thank you for saying that." Jasmine smiled again. She gave him a friendly shove.

"You're really pretty when you smile," Mark said. "You should do it more often."

"Well—"

Chapter 9

All of a sudden, Mark kissed her. She kissed him back. What a surprise! Mark's kiss was soft and gentle. Not at all rough and tough like how he was at school.

Mark put his arms around her. Jasmine did the same to him. She wasn't thinking. Then she was. She pulled away from him.

"Whoa!" she said, flustered. She also felt nervous. Excited. It all felt good.

"That was awesome," he said. He wasn't smiling.

"See you in school tomorrow," Jasmine said, turning down a street. Her house was minutes away. She felt herself blush.

"Maybe someday you'll let me walk you home," he called.

"Maybe," Jasmine called back. She didn't turn around. How could she look at him?

Then she did.

Mark was still standing there. Smiling.

"You're such a nerd," Jasmine said. Then she

turned around and continued walking. The sweet heat of the blush warmed her cheeks.

It was a few days later. Jasmine poured red sauce into cooked noodles.

Her mom was standing next to her in the kitchen. She was cutting up pieces of garlic bread. The kitchen wasn't big. It was cozy like the rest of the house.

Taylor Swift was playing. She wasn't Jasmine's favorite. But it was easier to do things when there was background noise.

"Dinner is just about ready," Jasmine said.

"Great," her mom said. She put the garlic bread on the table

There was a knock on the door.

"Are you expecting anyone?" Jasmine's mom asked as she went to answer the door.

"No."

For a second she thought it was Mark. They hadn't talked much since the kiss. They weren't exactly avoiding each other. But school was busy.

Chapter 9

And Jasmine didn't always see him after practice.

"Hey, Jasmine," a voice said. It was Officer Villa.

"Hey," she said.

"It smells great in here."

"Yeah. You want to eat with us?" she asked.

"Sorry, I can't."

Jasmine turned the flame down on dinner.

"I haven't been back to Wagner Park," she said. "We're practicing at Gomez Field."

"I'm not here about that." Officer Villa tried to smile. He looked uncomfortable. "It's about this game with the boys."

"What about it?" Jasmine said. She felt ready to fight. Girls could play football. She didn't always want to argue with people.

"You can't do it, Jasmine," he said. "Some of the boys' parents found out. They spoke to officials in city hall. They contacted my boss. People aren't ready for boys and girls to play tackle football together."

"What if we do it anyway?" she asked.

"The police will have to stop you." He motioned to Jasmine's mom. "Then it becomes an issue for your mom. It actually becomes an issue for all the parents. They're your legal guardians. They're responsible for you."

"So I can't play because I'm a kid?" Jasmine was upset. "All of our hard work is for nothing?" She turned away. Crying was useless. She was beginning to hate the word no.

"Not necessarily," her mom said. "You could bring this up to the city council."

Jasmine looked at Officer Villa.

"Sure," he agreed. "You could propose it. Ask them about forming a girls' tackle football team. You didn't hear that from me, though."

"But the team needs to practice. I need to coach. Is there even enough time?" She was starting to feel overwhelmed. "I mean, what's the big deal? All I … all we want to do is play football."

The adults stared at her.

Chapter 9

"I guess I need to do it," she said. "I need to take on Meadow Springs City Hall."

"Yes," Officer Villa said cautiously. "But the parents' minds seem made up. Some of them are on the city council. You'll need to address them carefully. They won't want to make other parents angry."

"They just don't want their boys to lose. Not to a bunch of girls," Jasmine said. "Because that's what would happen. They know it."

"Maybe." Officer Villa grinned. "You may be right, Jasmine. But right now that game can't happen."

CHAPTER 10

DOWN

"But you guys can't quit!" Jasmine said. She was talking to Kendra and Kim. It was just before practice. The whole team was there. "We've come so far! Kendra, you're lightning fast. I don't know anybody that can move like you do. And, Kim? You're a great kicker. We need you both on our team."

Jasmine stared at the girls. Then she realized something. The Chavez sisters were identical twins. But she saw how different they were.

"Our parents found out about the game,"

Kendra said. "Tom Kurtz told his mom. He's a Marauder. Then she called our mom."

"Everybody thinks we'll get hurt if we play the boys," Kim said.

"But you won't," Jasmine said.

"Tell them you're not going to play," Emma said.

"Yeah," Alejandra said. "Then play anyway."

"That's what I'm going to do," Lisa declared. "If they say anything."

"No!" Jasmine said sharply. "We don't want to lie. Do it the right way. Or nobody will take us seriously. They'll focus on the lie. Not the victory. We need to beat the boys. Fair and square."

"I say we call those boys out." Becky smirked. "Shame them into playing us."

"Nah," Jo-Jo said. "We shouldn't have to do that."

"Jo-Jo's right," Jasmine said. "There's going to be a meeting at city hall."

"About us?" Zoe asked.

Chapter 10

"We haven't told our parents about this game," Tess said nervously.

"Well, there's just a meeting about city stuff," Jasmine said. "But I'm going to bring this up. They're going see what we can do. Girls rule! We can do anything boys can. I can't force you guys to come. But, please. Will you come? City hall will know we mean business."

"I'll be there," Zoe said. "I might get grounded for a year. It'll be worth it."

"Me too," Tess said. "I don't need a social life. At least not till high school next year."

Emma, Becky, and Jo-Jo also said they would come.

"I like playing football," Ashlan said. "I think my parents will be surprised. But I won't get in trouble. I'll be there."

"You know something, Ash," Becky said. "For a nerd? You're pretty cool."

Becky gave Ashlan a warm hug. Everybody seemed a little surprised. Tough Becky was a hugger. At the same time, it seemed right. Over the past weeks they had become close. A team.

Alejandra and Lisa also said they would come.

All the eyes turned to Kendra and Kim.

"We understand, you guys—" Jasmine started to say.

"I will be there," Kim interrupted. "I'm part of this team."

"Me too." Kendra smiled. "I may not have talent. But I feel great when we're playing."

All the girls cheered. Then they started their practice.

"Bummer about the game," Mark said. He sat down next to Jasmine.

It was lunchtime. Jasmine was sitting at the lunch tables. She was working on what she was going to say at the city council meeting.

"Don't think you're off the hook yet," Jasmine said. "I'm taking this all the way to city hall. Tell your Marauders the game is still on."

"If anyone can do it, you can," Mark said. "What are you calling your team?"

"We don't have a name yet. We've been too busy prepping to beat you guys." Jasmine took a chip. She popped it into her mouth. Not the healthiest choice. But she wasn't hungry. She was too excited about the meeting.

"Do you want me to be there?" Mark asked. "At the council meeting, I mean."

"You *want* to be there?" Jasmine was shocked. Maybe Mark really liked her. Would that be so bad?

"Yeah," he said. "For moral support."

"Okay." Jasmine had to stop thinking about Mark as boyfriend material. She didn't want him to know she like-liked him. "You could be there representing the Marauders. In case they want you to talk. You'll probably just say something lame, though." She was used to being at odds with him. Saying something nice would feel weird.

"I won't say anything lame." He looked

around campus. "But I will come to the meeting. To be there for you, just so you know."

Jasmine grinned. Mark was really cute. So many girls would be stoked if he had said that to them. "Is this some mind game you're playing?" she asked.

"Mind game?" Mark seemed confused.

"You're trying to make me soft. You're trying to make me like you more. This way I'll take it easy on you during the game." Jasmine eyed Mark. She wanted him to know she was serious.

Mark stared right back. Then he cracked up. "Like I told you. Not everything is a competition, Jasmine." He stood up. "I like you. What can I say? I've got great taste."

Jasmine stared at him.

Mark wasn't smiling anymore. He was serious. Then Mark's smirk returned. "And besides, whether I like you or not? I'm not giving you any breaks come game day." Then he walked away.

Jasmine watched him go. He went up to his friends. She watched them fist bump.

She wondered what he would tell them about her. Then Jasmine realized she didn't care. Mark made her feel good. That was what was important.

She went back to her notes. City hall was not ready for her. She was going to let them have it.

CHAPTER 11

EXTRA POINTS

Jasmine's mom was making dinner. Jasmine could smell it as she walked in. Practice had gone well that day. The girls worked on strategy. Jasmine taught them different plays. She didn't freak out if they messed up. Regular coaches would drill and drill and drill. Jasmine didn't. She wanted the girls to like football. Hopefully they could put it all together.

"You got a letter," her mom said. She was making fried rice. There was corn soup on the stove. Jasmine loved corn soup. "It's on the table. Looks pretty official."

It was from the Pop Warner Association. They ran youth football leagues. Jasmine opened the letter. As she read it, she felt excitement. And fear.

"Pop Warner is starting a girls' football league," Jasmine said. "They want me to help organize a team here."

Her mom looked up from the stovetop. "Really?" she said.

Jasmine sat down at the kitchen table. The plates and bowls were already out. She looked at the letter. "It's going to be an all-girls' league," Jasmine said.

"So, you won. You and the other girls can play football." Her mom put some fried rice on each plate. She also ladled some soup.

"Yeah," Jasmine said. She put the letter on the table.

"Why don't you seem happy? Isn't that what this is all about?" Her mom started to eat.

"I *am* happy," Jasmine said. "I just … I don't know. I wasn't expecting this."

"Do you think it's too much pressure? Does Pop Warner make it too official?"

"No. I was gearing up for a fight. Then the game. This seems fake. Like they want us to go away."

It was the next day. The girls gathered for practice.

"I'm starting a Pop Warner girls' league," Jasmine said. "After we beat the boys."

All of the girls stared at her.

"Huh? Why do we still need to play them? Didn't you just want to play football?" Zoe asked.

"This isn't about me. It's not about what I want," Jasmine said. "It's about all of us. We could play against girls. But you saw how the boys treated us."

"Isn't one of them Mark?" Becky asked. "Your boyfriend?"

The other girls giggled.

"He's not my boyfriend." Jasmine blushed. "Not yet, anyway."

Tess and Zoe smirked.

"Remember how mean their coach was?" Jasmine went on. "We mentioned playing on his team. Coach looked at us like we were nuts. We will fight this our whole lives. Girls aren't as good as boys. That's what they'll say. Girls aren't as capable. It will be worse if we don't stand up for ourselves. And fight it now."

"She's right," Jo-Jo said excitedly. "We need to kick some boy butt!"

Everyone cheered.

"After this game, we might never get to play boys again," Jasmine said. "We might only play girls. That's okay, I guess. But I want us to have this chance. To beat the boys at their own game."

"I have a question," Tess said, raising her hand. "What is our team called?"

Everyone looked at Jasmine.

"How about the Underdogs?" Lisa suggested.

Chapter 11

The girls thought about it. Then they started nodding their heads.

"That's perfect," Becky said. "Because we're going to show everyone. We are anything but underdogs!"

Everyone cheered.

"Well, Lisa," Jasmine said. "Looks like we're the Underdogs."

CHAPTER 12

SHOWDOWN

Jasmine was at city hall. The meeting room was packed. The room had a long table in front. There were three chairs behind it. Three microphones were on top. A podium faced the table. There was a microphone there too.

I guess that's where I'll be standing, Jasmine thought.

Behind the podium were rows of seats. There were many rows. It looked like a movie theater.

How many people came to city council meetings? Jasmine didn't know. But today there was a crowd. She felt nervous.

Mayor Rice sat in the middle of the long table. Jasmine thought she looked serious. One council member sat on either side. One man and one woman. They all looked serious too.

A man in a suit stood at the podium. He talked about water rates. Jasmine knew she should pay attention. But she couldn't.

The girls from the Underdogs were there. So were their parents. The Marauders were there too. And they had brought their parents.

Other people were there. Who were they? Were they there because of the football game? Boy versus girl was a big deal. A photographer carried a big camera.

Wow! Now she was super-nervous.

"You know what you want to say?" her mom asked. She pointed to Jasmine's notes.

Chapter 12

"Yeah, I think," Jasmine said. She tried not to wrinkle her papers.

Eventually, the suit stepped away from the mic.

"Is there any new business?" Mayor Rice asked.

"Yes," Jasmine said. She popped up from her seat.

There were cheers from her team.

"Please," Mayor Rice said. "Come to the podium."

Jasmine made her way over.

"Please keep this polite," Mayor Rice said to the crowd. "Everyone will have a turn to speak."

"So you want to play a football game," a council member said. "Against boys."

Whoa! The city council already knew the topic.

"Yes," Jasmine said.

There were cheers again.

"It seems unfair. Why can't we play coed football?" Jasmine looked at her notes. "What more do we have to prove? Women can do anything men can do. Serve in the military. Run major corporations. Lead cities and towns." Then she looked up. Jasmine looked at the two women before her. "I think you ladies would agree."

This got a big a cheer. The three-member city council smiled.

"Some people think girls shouldn't play coed football. But did you know this? The American Academy of Pediatrics says cheerleading causes the most injuries to high school girls." Jasmine made sure to make eye contact. "Women continue to fight for equality. With every victory there is a loss. You will decide what happens here. But you can't stop the tide. There will be coed football eventually. Here, and in other towns. Why can't we make this game happen first? Let's be leaders."

All eyes were on Jasmine. She felt her team's good energy.

Jasmine put her notes down. She stared at the mayor. "Mayor Rice, didn't you become mayor to

Chapter 12

make a difference? Will anything change because you are mayor? With respect, isn't that why you ran for office? To make positive changes?"

Everyone for coed football cheered.

"Please let the Underdogs play the Marauders. Give us the chance. We can do this. We won't disappoint. We won't embarrass you. Thank you."

"Thank you, Miss Le," Mayor Rice said. "That was a passionate speech. But we need to hear both sides."

A parent stepped forward. She said why she thought girls should not play coed.

Jasmine went back to her seat.

Several more opponents spoke.

"Thank you," Mayor Rice said. "I think we've heard enough. The council will discuss off mic."

The council members talked. Their mics were off. Nobody could hear.

"We're going to take a break," Mayor Rice said. The city council stepped out of the room.

Mark motioned Jasmine to the back.

Jasmine hugged Zoe, Tess, and the other girls. She made her way to Mark.

"You did a great job," Mark said.

"What do you think will happen?" Jasmine asked.

"I think they'll say yes."

"Really?" How could he be so sure? Jasmine wasn't.

"Yeah. You were pretty convincing."

The council returned. They took their seats. Everybody sat. The room was quiet.

"There was some debate," Mayor Rice said. "We looked at the pros. And the cons. The game can go forward. It will be Underdogs against Marauders."

All the girls screamed. They cheered, "Underdogs! Underdogs!"

Boys yelled, "Marauders! Marauders!"

Jasmine couldn't believe it. She looked at her

Chapter 12

teammates. Mark smiled. Then Jasmine looked at her mom. Her mom glowed with pride.

"Thank you! Mayor Rice, thank you," Jasmine said quietly. She gave the mayor a thumbs-up.

The Underdogs would play the Marauders. Would they win? Or lose?

Whatever happened, Jasmine Le felt victorious. All girls had won that night.

CHAPTER 13

ANY GIVEN SATURDAY

The Underdogs were the talk of the town. Everyone thought about the upcoming game.

Some parents still had a problem with it. They didn't want their boys to play. Coach Sanderson had more than enough players. So it didn't matter if some dropped out.

A local bakery sponsored the girls' uniforms.

"You ladies are doing something great," their sponsor said. "Show everybody there's nothing you can't do."

After the council meeting, many more girls wanted to play. The team decided they would add players. But only after the game.

"It's too close," Jasmine had said. "We're a tight-knit team. It takes time to train. Time to feel like a family. We'll add more players, for sure."

It was game day.

"Wow!" Jasmine said. "This is it."

She and the other girls walked onto the field.

"These new uniforms are the bomb," Tess gushed.

The game was at the high school. The stands were full. There were posters everywhere.

"Girls Rock!"

"Boys Rule, Girls Drool."

"Girl Power!"

"This is awesome," Zoe said. "Look at all these people. Who says you can't fight city hall?"

The game captivated the town. It was the

event of the year. All because Jasmine Le wouldn't take no for an answer.

"All right, huddle up!" Jasmine yelled.

She turned away from the crowd. "Stay focused. Stay on point," she said to herself.

The Underdogs gathered around her. It was the first huddle.

"Look, I really want to win. We all do," said Jasmine. "There's one rule. No matter what happens today. Have fun!"

The team cheered.

"Get those boys!" Jo-Jo yelled.

"Show everybody. Girls deserve to play football!" Kendra yelled.

"There's more to us than they know!" Kim yelled.

"And we're doing it as a team!" Becky yelled.

"Underdogs on three," Emma cheered.

Jasmine loved it. This was her team. And every player was equally important. Each player stacked her hand in the center of the huddle. They were ready.

"One, two, three," Jasmine called.

"Underdogs!" they yelled.

The Marauders stood on one side of the field. The Underdogs stood on the other. Jasmine and Mark were on the field. Between them was a referee. He held a coin. The ref would flip it. The winner would decide

"What side?" he asked Jasmine.

"Heads." She didn't take her eyes off Mark. He smiled at her.

The referee flipped the coin. It soared high. Then it landed. And bounced.

"Heads!" the referee called. "Underdogs decide."

The girls cheered. Jasmine smirked. Mark nodded his head.

CHAPTER 14

OFFENSE

The girls' team won the toss. They chose to take the ball. Play offense.

Boys played defense. Gabriel kicked the ball with everything he had. It flew threw the air. The crowd held its breath. The ball bounced. Then Ashlan picked it up. She started running down the field.

The boys charged toward her. Ashlan didn't get far. The Marauders defense tackled her.

Ashlan went down. Some roared with approval. Some gasped.

"Ashlan!" Jasmine cried. She ran over.

Everybody gathered around her. Ashlan lay on the field. She looked as flat as a pancake.

"Give her some space!" the ref called.

Ashlan quickly sat up. Then she got off the ground.

"Are you okay?" the ref asked.

"Yeah. It was just a tackle." Ashlan eyed the Marauders. "Are you guys okay?"

"Yeah, I'm fine," one guy said. "You took that hit good."

"Why are you surprised?" Ashlan asked, smiling.

The game was on!

The Underdogs remained on offense. Kendra and Zoe were wide receivers. Tess was a fullback. Kim was a halfback. Becky, Jo-Jo, Emma, Alejandra, and Lisa were on the offensive line. Alejandra was center. Lisa and Emma were guards. Becky and Jo-Jo were tackles. Ashlan was a tight end. Jasmine was the quarterback.

They had moved the ball to the twenty-yard line. The Marauders didn't seem able to stop them.

"Are they letting us?" Zoe asked between plays. "Like after that first tackle, they got nervous?"

"I hope not," Tess said.

So did Jasmine. She wanted to beat the boys. It had to be fair and square.

The ball was put in play again. The boys advanced. They moved forward with speed. They looked more determined.

Zoe was right! Jasmine thought.

Jasmine moved back. The boys were fast. But they had left Zoe wide open. Jasmine pulled back her arm. Then she hurled the ball. It was a perfect spiral.

Time seemed to stand still.

The crowd was silent.

Zoe held up her hands. The ball slid right into them. She took off. Then crossed the end zone.

The Underdogs had scored! It was the first touchdown.

"I don't believe it!" Coach Sanderson yelled. "Do not let them score. We cannot lose! Stop taking it easy, guys."

Could they score an extra point? The kick was set up. The players moved into position.

Kim was the kicker. She ran toward the ball. The kick was good!

The score was 7–0. Go, Underdogs!

Mark smiled at Jasmine. It was a nice smile. "Let's play some football," it seemed to say.

It was the second quarter. The Marauders turned things around. They played a tougher game. Their offense showed no mercy. The team easily got to the ten-yard line.

Mark threw the ball to the tight end. Touchdown! Then they won the extra point. The game was now tied. Both teams had seven points.

Jasmine got a sinking feeling.

The Underdogs had started off strong. They

had scored right away. Then the Marauders started to take things seriously.

Jasmine looked at her teammates. Their mouths were open. They were sweating. Everyone was tired.

She eyed the clock. Two minutes before halftime. "Time out!" Jasmine called.

The girls looked at her.

The ref blew his whistle. "Time!" he yelled.

The girls huddled up.

"Ladies," Jasmine said. "I know we're tired. It's almost halftime."

"Yeah," said Becky. "So let's just get there."

"You're all playing awesome," Jasmine said. "Keep it up. Have fun!"

"Underdogs on three," Jo-Jo said.

"Underdogs!" they yelled with energy.

The boys hiked the ball. Mark threw it to the Marauders fullback.

Kendra intercepted. She ran down the field. The Marauders chased after her. The Underdogs tried to protect her. One of the Marauders got close. Kendra was too fast.

She passed the fifty-yard line. The forty-yard line. The thirty-yard line. Before anybody could take another breath, Kendra scored.

Kim kicked the ball. It was good! The clock ran out. Halftime.

The score was 14–7 for the Underdogs.

The girls rested. Drank water. Wiped away the sweat.

Then halftime was over.

The ball didn't budge. Both teams seemed worn out.

"Come on!" Coach Sanderson screamed. "Stop! You're giving up the ball."

Neither team scored in the third quarter.

"Jasmine," Zoe said. It was the fourth quarter. "We might win this thing!"

Jasmine smiled. She nodded her head. Were the boys trying to trick them again? Were they really

Chapter 14

that tired? She got her answer with the next play.

She threw the ball to Tess. Tess fumbled.

Mark swooped in out of nowhere. He picked up the ball. Then tore off down the field.

He easily passed Becky, Jo-Jo, everyone. Nobody could stop him.

The stands erupted. "Go, Marauders," fans screamed. Touchdown!

Then their kicker scored the extra point.

It was a tie, 14–14.

In the next play, the Marauders kicked the ball. Jo-Jo caught it. But she barely got down the field. The Marauders tackled her easily.

Nobody seemed nervous when the girls got tackled anymore. But the Underdogs looked spent. They were falling apart. They'd never played a game like this before.

The Marauders switched out players. There was no way the Underdogs would last if the game went into overtime.

Jasmine eyed the clock. Less than two minutes to go. "Time!" she called.

This was their last time out. The girls huddled up. They were tired. Their uniforms were filthy.

"Okay, you guys," Jasmine said. "You've played great. Thank you. For everything you've done. Not only for the team, but also for me. As your coach or whatever I am."

The girls stared at her. Their mouths hung open. Sweat dripped from their faces.

"Let's put these guys away," she said.

"Underdogs on three," Alejandra called.

"Underdogs!" they all yelled. They got back in the line.

"Hut one, hut two, hut three!" Jasmine called.

The ball was in play again.

The Marauders stormed toward them. They easily got past the Underdogs offensive line.

Jasmine looked for Zoe, Tess, Ashlan. Somebody. Anybody. Who could catch the ball?

Nobody was open. The Marauders were all

over them. In seconds they would be coming for her. She took off running.

Jasmine ran faster than she ever had in her life. She spun around players. She jumped through the air to avoid the boys. She kept running. The forty-yard line flew by. Then she passed the thirty-yard line.

Jasmine could feel the boys at her heels.

She was hot. Tired. But she moved faster. A few of the boys fell at her feet. They had just missed tackling her.

Jasmine crossed the ten-yard line. She was only feet from a touchdown. She could taste it!

Then Mark came out of nowhere. He started to wrap his arms around her. Jasmine jumped through his arms. She toppled over the end zone. The clock ran out.

The Underdogs had won!

The crowd rushed the field. There were loud cheers for both teams.

Jasmine sprang to her feet. She ran over to her teammates. They hugged. Then the girls lifted

Jasmine into the air. When she came down, the Underdogs continued cheering.

"Man, Jasmine," Mark said when it calmed down. "You are tough."

"I'm just glad I fell in the right direction."

"You were right all along," Mark said. "Girls can do anything boys can do."

"It's a good thing you learned now." She patted him on the shoulder. "Your life is going to be a lot easier."

"I doubt you'd ever make my life easy," Mark said, laughing.

"Not a chance."

They hugged.

Jasmine turned and continued cheering with her team. Victory felt good.

CHAPTER 15

UNDERDOGS RULE

It was a few days after the game. There was another meeting at city hall. People were still in awe. The girls had won a tackle football game against the boys.

The girls stood on the main stage. Every seat in the hall was filled. People were standing in the back. Some were sitting in the aisles. Reporters and photographers were there.

"We are here to celebrate some girls. Let's recognize their achievement." It was Mayor Rice. She spoke into a microphone. "Meadow Springs celebrates each of you. Here is a trophy for your victory. For believing in yourselves."

Everybody cheered.

The city council handed out trophies. The trophies were shaped like footballs. Each Underdog got one.

"The Pop Warner league told me," Mayor Rice said. "That Jasmine Le will start coed football teams. The new teams will take over our existing league. Pop Warner after-school football will be coed!"

There were more cheers.

The mayor looked at Jasmine. She held out the mic. Jasmine got nervous. She waved the mic away.

"Say something, Jasmine!" Mark called. "Are you scared?"

Jasmine looked at Zoe and Tess. They both motioned her toward the microphone.

She took the mic from the mayor. "Well," she said. "Thank you. This is such an honor. I know my teammates agree with me. We would play football no matter what. Even if we had lost the big game."

The crowd roared.

"But fun is more important than winning. We loved beating the boys. But we played for fun."

The Underdogs cheered.

"And now there's the new coed league. It won't be just a girls' league. That is so cool! We're going to have even more fun!"

People clapped. Yelled. Stomped their feet.

Jasmine looked at her mom. She smiled. Jasmine smiled back.

"None of this would have been possible," Jasmine said. She looked at her teammates. "Without the support of our families. And without our team coming together. I love you guys!"

The cheers continued.

The Underdogs hugged. The girls were underdogs no more.

WANT TO KEEP READING?

9781680211078

Turn the page for a sneak peek at another book in the White Lightning series:

GRAND SLAM

CHAPTER 1

MATCH POINT

Brad Kingsley wiped the sweat from his brow. He watched his opponent. The boy spun his tennis racket around in his hand. Then he hit the ball against the ground a few times.

"Oh, come on! Don't stall!" Brad whispered. He didn't want anyone to hear him. Brad didn't speak to people like that.

His muscles tensed. Brad hated this part of the game. He knew his opponent was trying to mess with him.

The score was 20–40. His opponent had to score one more point. Brad would lose the match.

Brad had started off well. He'd scored the first two points. Then his mind drifted. He started thinking about other things. Could his opponent sense this? Brad wondered if that was why he was losing now.

Why do I keep playing this game? I can't even focus on it, he thought.

Brad was a sophomore at Valley High School. He had been playing tennis since he was ten. Brad was sixteen now. Varsity tennis was competitive. He was really good.

You play tennis because you're good at it, he told himself. He was trying to pump himself up. It was a trick Coach Kennedy had taught. She was the varsity coach.

Brad was tall and in shape. He had an athletic build. His hair was blond. Brad's green eyes were light.

Chapter 1

His biggest challenge was concentration. Brad found it hard. His parents told him he had an auditory processing disorder. Something about his ears and brain not being in sync. He didn't know what that meant. But sometimes he lost his train of thought. It happened a lot when people talked to him. If they didn't say too much, Brad was okay. But sometimes Brad would get confused.

When that happened, he had a few tricks. He would either nod his head, or say nothing. The other person didn't realize they had lost him. He had another trick too. Brad repeated the last thing said to him. He could process the words better this way.

He was a good student. He had math, English, history, biology, and PE. PE was tennis practice. His elective was a resource class. It was not his elective by choice.

Resource was like study hall. Brad's teacher was Mr. Cohen. He was tall. The teacher had a loud voice. But with Brad, Mr. Cohen spoke softly.

Mr. Cohen was from New York. He had an accent. Brad liked it. He liked asking the teacher questions about New York. They chatted when Brad's work was done. The teacher or an aide often helped Brad with his work. After resource class, most of his assignments were done.

Brad didn't like what kids called the resource room. They said it was the "dumb class." Aside from the cruel words, being in resource was fine.

Brad's mind was not on his game.

What should I do later?

Ugh. He was doing it again. His concentration was drifting.

He stared at his opponent. Brad looked at the crowd. There weren't many people. But there were enough for Brad.

He started to think about the heat. His homework. Then he saw his parents. They were sitting in the crowd. Were they looking at him?

Chapter 1

His mom was smiling. His dad was serious. Like he wanted to say "Stay focused, Brad!"

People always said that to him. Sometimes it bugged him. Staying focused was often out of his control.

He also saw some kids he didn't know well. He'd noticed them at school.

Brad's eyes focused on a girl. She had long black hair. Her skin was a light olive color. She had dark brown eyes.

The girl smiled at him. The smile seemed to say "I believe in you."

Brad couldn't stop looking at her.

That's when he heard a popping sound.